COSMO
for Captain

Jonathan
Emmett

Illustrated by
Peter Rutherford

OXFORD
UNIVERSITY PRESS

Great Clarendon Street, Oxford OX2 6DP

Oxford University Press is a department of the University of Oxford.
It furthers the University's objective of excellence in research, scholarship,
and education by publishing worldwide in

Oxford   New York

Auckland   Cape Town   Dar es Salaam   Hong Kong   Karachi
Kuala Lumpur   Madrid   Melbourne   Mexico City   Nairobi
New Delhi   Shanghai   Taipei   Toronto

With offices in

Argentina   Austria   Brazil   Chile   Czech Republic   France   Greece
Guatemala   Hungary   Italy   Japan   Poland   Portugal   Singapore
South Korea   Switzerland   Thailand   Turkey   Ukraine   Vietnam

Oxford is a registered trade mark of Oxford University Press
in the UK and in certain other countries

British Library Cataloguing in Publication Data

Data available

ISBN 978-0-19-915162-2

17 19 20 18 16

Mixed Pack (1 of 6 different titles): ISBN 978-0-19-915160-8
Class Pack (6 copies of 6 titles): ISBN 978-0-19-915159-2

Printed in China by Imago

Oxford OWL Discover eBooks, inspirational
resources, advice and support
www.oxfordowl.co.uk

Contents

Chapter 1

Boulder Ball

It was a sunny afternoon in Volcano Valley. The dinosaurs had met next to the lake. They were going to play boulder ball. Steggs and Tricky were the team captains.

"I want to be a captain," squeaked Cosmo. He was the smallest dinosaur.

"Don't be silly," laughed the others.
"You're not big enough."

"It shouldn't matter how big I am!"
said Cosmo.

The dinosaurs stood in a line.
The captains picked teams.
Cosmo and Patty were picked last.
Nobody wanted them.
Cosmo was too small.
And Patty was too slow.

The captains chose a boulder.
Then the game began.

Cosmo and Patty tried to get the
boulder. They tried very hard.
Patty ran after it. But she was too slow.
Someone else always got there first.

Cosmo could get to the boulder. But he was too small. He couldn't move it – no matter how hard he tried. The other dinosaurs laughed at him.

"It's not fair," said Cosmo. "If I were captain, I'd choose a small boulder. One that everyone could play with."

Just then, a dreadful roar echoed
across the valley.

"Oh, no!" wailed Steggs. "It's Tyro!"

Tyro was a terrible tyrannosaur. She
was always gobbling up other dinosaurs.

"Quick!" shrieked Tricky. "We'd better
hide – or she will eat us."

The dinosaurs ran off. Patty and
Cosmo were left by the lake.

Patty was very scared. She was too big
to hide and too slow to run. Her large
eyes filled with tears.

"Don't wait for me, Cosmo," she said
sadly. "You had better go and hide."

Cosmo was scared too. But he stuck by
his friend and thought fast.

"Don't worry," he said.
"We'll be all right."

Chapter 2

Shake, Rattle, and Roar!

The ground shook and the lake shivered
as Tyro stomped into the valley.
    Her claws were dripping with blood.

She had already eaten two
megalosaurs that morning.
   But they were just a snack.
Now she was ready for a proper meal.
   "DINNER TIME!" she roared.

Tyro arrived at the lake, but there was no
one there. Even Patty had disappeared!

Tyro was not stupid. She knew the dinosaurs were hiding. And she knew how to find them.

"What shall I have to eat?" she said, as if thinking out loud. "A juicy iguanodon? Or a fat triceratops? No! What I REALLY fancy is a crunchy STEGOSAURUS!"

The dinosaurs were hiding behind a pile of rocks.

Steggs heard Tyro say that she was going to eat him. He was very, very scared.

He trembled so much that the plates on his back were rattling.

"Shush," whispered the other dinosaurs. "Tyro will hear you."

But it was too late. Tyro was already coming towards them.

Tyro had almost reached the pile of rocks, when she heard a squeaky voice.

"Hey, SWAMP-BREATH! If you want to pick on someone, why not pick on me?"

Tyro looked round and saw Cosmo. He was dancing up and down next to the lake.

15

"Don't be silly," snorted Tyro. "I wouldn't waste my time chasing you. *You* are only a little mouthful."

And she turned back towards the rocks.

Chapter 3

Scaredy-saurus Rex

Tyro had almost found the other
dinosaurs, when Cosmo called out again.

"You tyrannosaurs are all the same,"
he said. "If someone stands up
to you – you run off with your tail
between your legs."

Tyro stopped in her tracks.

"WHAT DID YOU SAY?" she snarled.

"You heard me," yelled Cosmo.
"You're a SCAREDY-SAURUS!"

"THAT'S ENOUGH!" shouted Tyro "I'll
show you who's a scaredy-saurus."
The tyrannosaur swung around and
stormed towards the lake.

Cosmo did not look frightened. But he
was just pretending. He was really very
scared.

Tyro's huge jaws swooped down.

It looked as if he was going to be snapped up! He was going to be chewed into a thousand soggy pieces!

But Cosmo didn't run away!

At the last moment, Cosmo jumped backwards into the lake.

He landed on a small island, close to the shore.

"Come on, CLUMSY-CLAWS," he yelled. "Come and get me. If you dare."

Tyro hesitated. She didn't like water. But the island was very close to the shore.

"Hey, FOSSIL-FACE. What's the matter?" shouted Cosmo. He waved his tiny fists. "Are you a scaredy-saurus after all?"

That settled it.

Tyro wasn't going to be called any more names. She charged into the water and waded towards the island.

The other dinosaurs peered out from their hiding place. They were amazed by what was happening.

"What does Cosmo think he's doing?" asked Tricky. "Has he gone mad?"

"And where is Patty?" asked Steggs.

Tyro thrashed through the water towards Cosmo.

The little dinosaur was still laughing. The more Cosmo laughed, the madder Tyro got. She was so mad, she didn't notice that Cosmo's island was MOVING.

It was leading her further and further into the lake.

Chapter 4

Patty Pops Up

All of a sudden, Tyro was up to her neck in water.

"HELP! HELP! I CAN'T SWIM!" she shrieked.

"Oh, dear," said Cosmo. He wasn't scared any more. "I don't suppose you want my help. I'm only a *little mouthful.*"

"PLEASE!" howled Tyro. "I'll do anything you want."

"Anything?" asked Cosmo.

"Anything," spluttered Tyro.

"Do you promise to leave our valley and never come back?"

"Yes! Yes! I promise," gurgled Tyro. She was desperate. "Just get me out of this water."

"All right, then," said Cosmo.
He stamped his foot on the island.
Patty's head popped out of the water
next to him.

Then, everyone realized what had
happened.

Cosmo wasn't standing on a real
island. He was standing on Patty's back!

That was how she had disappeared.
That was why the island had been
moving.

Patty dragged Tyro back to the shore.

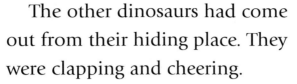

The other dinosaurs had come
out from their hiding place. They
were clapping and cheering.

Tyro felt terrible. And she hated being
laughed at. She struggled to her feet.

Then she trudged out of the valley,
without saying a word.

The dinosaurs thanked Cosmo and
Patty for saving them.

"I thought I was going to be eaten,"
said Steggs.

"I would never have dared to lead Tyro
into the lake," said Tricky.

"It was all Cosmo's idea," said Patty. "He's the one you should thank."

"Nonsense," said Cosmo. "I could never have done it without Patty. It was just good teamwork."

"Now, what happened to our game of boulder ball?" asked Cosmo.

"I think we should start again," said Steggs.

"With new captains," said Tricky.

"Someone who will look after their whole team," agreed Steggs.

"COSMO AND PATTY!" shouted all
the others.

About the author

I made up this story when I was seventeen. I was asked to tell a dinosaur story at a cub-scout camp-fire.

Instead of using a story from a book, I made one up and drew lots of large pictures to go with it.

The story worked well and, years later, I wrote it down to make this book.

You can find out more about Jonathan Emmett's books by visiting his website at
www.scribblestreet.co.uk